For Isla, Harry and Bethany
D.C.
For Fox
C.F.

First published in 2015 by Nosy Crow Ltd

The Crow's Nest, 10a Lant Street

London SE1 1QR

www.nosycrow.com

ISBN 978 0 85763 339 2 (HB)

ISBN 978 0 85763 340 8 (PB)

Nosy Crow and associated logos are trademark

and/or registered trademarks of Nosy Crow Ltd.

A CIP catalogue record for this book is available from the British Library.

Printed in China

Papers used by Nosy Crow are made from wood grown in sustainable forests.

1 3 5 7 9 8 6 4 2 (HB)

1 3 5 7 9 8 6 4 2 (PB)

A Lullaby for Little One

Dawn Casey

Illustrated by Charles Fuge

nosy crow

Down in the woods in the late evening sun,
Big Daddy Rabbit said,

"Come,
Little One!"

"Let's race and let's chase,
and let's laugh and let's leap!

We'll have lots of fun,
then you must go to sleep."

So, they **raced** and they **chased** . . .

. . . and they shouted, "Woo-hoo!"

They whooped and they swooped . . .
and Owl called,
"Twit-tu-woo!"

They played
hide-and-seek . . .

. . . and found Mouse,

"Peek-a-boo!"

They splashed
and they sploshed . . .

. . . and then Bear
joined in, too!

The last of the sun warmed the big happy crew.
They danced and they shouted
and all sang,

"Ya-hooOOOO!"

They **whirled** and they **twirled**
with a **laugh** and a **leap** . . .

. . . 'til they tumbled
and rolled in a glorious heap.

But . . .

. . . Little One suddenly whimpered,

"BOO-HOOOOOO!"

And Big Daddy Rabbit said,
"What a to-do!"

"Was that all too much of
a hullaballoo?
I think that it's time for
a lullaballoo."

So Big Rabbit swayed
in the slow-setting sun,
as he hugged and he hummed,

"Hush-a-bye,
Little One."

Baby snuffled
and snuggled.
They both curled up tight.

"I love you, my Little One,
sweet dreams, good night."